the Gingerbread man

for my niece Nicki
love, C. J.

First American edition 2002
Originally published in Australia by HarperCollins*Publishers*
Pty Limited as an Angus & Robertson book.

www.houghtonmifflinbooks.com

Library of Congress Cataloging-in-Publication Data
Jones, Carol.
   The gingerbread man / Carol Jones. — 1st American ed.
      p. cm.
   Summary: A freshly baked gingerbread man escapes when he is taken out of the oven
and eludes a series of nursery rhyme characters who hope to eat him until meeting up
with a clever fox. Includes recipe.
   ISBN 0-618-18822-3
      1. Toy and moveable books—Specimens. [1. Fairy tales. 2. Folklore. 3. Toy and moveable
books.] I. Gingerbread boy. English. II. Title.

PZ8.J534 Gi 2002
398.2 — dc21
[E]   2001039258

Printed In China
10 9 8 7 6 5 4 3 2 1

the Gingerbread man

CAROL JONES

Houghton Mifflin Company Boston 2002

Walter Lorraine Books

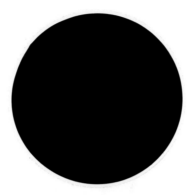

Once upon a time a little old woman and a little old man lived together in a little old house. One morning the little old woman decided to make a gingerbread man.

In a large bowl she mixed all the ingredients together with a wooden spoon. Next she rolled out the dough, carefully cut out the shape of a little man and popped him into the oven to bake.

When the little old woman thought that the gingerbread man was cooked, she opened the oven door. Out jumped the gingerbread man and away he ran out of the kitchen and down the street.

As he ran he shouted ...

"Run, run as fast as you can,

You can't catch me,

I'm the gingerbread man."

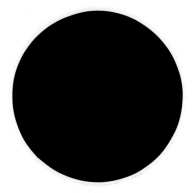

Humpty Dumpty had been sitting on the wall for a long time and he was feeling so hungry that he nearly toppled off the wall. When he saw the gingerbread man running past he called out:

"Stop, stop, gingerbread man. You look tasty to eat."

However, the gingerbread man only laughed, and as he ran faster he called back:

"I have run away from a little old woman and a little old man,

And I can run away from you, I can."

"Run, run as fast as you can,

You can't catch me,

I'm the gingerbread man."

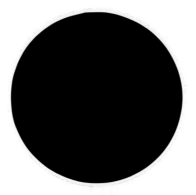

Little Boy Blue was having a lovely sleep in the haystack.
Then he was awakened by the sheep bleating and the cows mooing
at the gingerbread man who was running past.
When Little Boy Blue saw the gingerbread man he said:

"Stop, stop, gingerbread man. I need some breakfast."

The gingerbread man just laughed and as he ran faster he called back:

*"I have run away from a little old woman and a little old man
and Humpty Dumpty,*

And I can run away from you, I can."

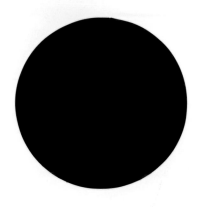

"*Run, run as fast as you can,*

You can't catch me,

I'm the gingerbread man."

The Old Woman Who Lived in a Shoe was wondering what to give her children for tea, when she spied the gingerbread man racing past. She called out:

"Stop, stop, gingerbread man. You will make a fine meal for my hungry children."

The gingerbread man just laughed and as he ran faster he called back:

"I have run away from a little old woman and a little old man and Humpty Dumpty and Little Boy Blue,

And I can run away from you, I can."

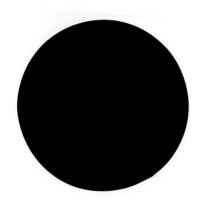

"*Run, run as fast as you can,*

You can't catch me,

I'm the gingerbread man."

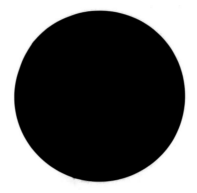

The Grand Old Duke of York was feeling very tired and hungry
after marching his soldiers up and down the hill all day.
When he noticed the gingerbread man racing past he said:

"Stop, stop, gingerbread man. I haven't eaten all day long.
I am so hungry that my stomach is rumbling."

The gingerbread man just laughed and as he ran faster he called back:

"I have run away from a little old woman and a little old man and
Humpty Dumpty and Little Boy Blue and The Old Woman
Who Lived in a Shoe,

And I can run away from you, I can."

"Run, run as fast as you can,

You can't catch me,

I'm the gingerbread man."

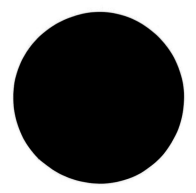

Little Miss Muffet had finished eating her curds and whey.
When she saw the gingerbread man racing past she said:

"Stop, stop, gingerbread man. You will make a delicious dessert."

The gingerbread man just laughed and as he ran faster he called back:

*"I have run away from a little old woman and a little old man and
Humpty Dumpty and Little Boy Blue and The Old Woman
Who Lived in a Shoe and the Grand Old Duke of York,*

And I can run away from you, I can."

"Run, run as fast as you can,

You can't catch me,

I'm the gingerbread man."

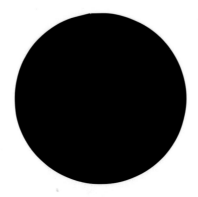

The gingerbread man ran on until he came to a river
but he didn't know how to cross. A sly fox came along and said:

"Do you want to cross the river?"

"Yes, I do. I don't want to be eaten," said the gingerbread man.

"Then jump on my back and I'll take you across," said the fox.

So the gingerbread man jumped on the fox's back and the fox began
to swim across the river. When the fox came to the other side, he said:

"Jump onto my head. Then you can easily step onto the bank."

Now the gingerbread man climbed onto the fox's head.

With a flick of his head the hungry fox tossed the gingerbread man into the air, and . . .

You can make your own delicious gingerbread man by following this recipe.
Ask an adult to help you.

Apart from the following ingredients, you will need these implements:

A teaspoon, a tablespoon, a wooden spoon, measuring cups, a small saucepan, a sieve,
2 bowls, a rolling pin, a gingerbread man cookie-cutter or a knife, an oven tray, oven mitts

INGREDIENTS

3 tablespoons molasses

2 cups plain flour

1 teaspoon baking soda

3 teaspoons ground ginger

125 g (4 oz) butter or margarine

⅓ cup soft brown sugar

1 egg yolk

5 currants

1 glacé cherry

METHOD

1. Preheat the oven. If you have a gas cooker: 180° Celsius (350° Fahrenheit). If you have an electric cooker: 190–200° Celsius (375–400° Fahrenheit).

2. Warm the molasses in a small saucepan. Use a gentle heat.

3. Place the sieve over a large bowl, and sift together the flour, baking soda and ground ginger. Set aside.

4. Cream the butter and sugar together in a medium-size bowl until the butter–sugar mixture is fluffy, then add the egg yolk and mix well.

5. Gradually add the butter–sugar mixture and the warmed molasses to the sifted dry ingredients, and mix well.

6. Turn the mixture onto a lightly floured surface, knead lightly and roll out to about 3 mm (⅓") thickness.

7. If you don't have a gingerbread man cookie-cutter, use your hands or a knife to shape the gingerbread man.

8. Use currants for eyes and buttons, and a piece of glacé cherry for nose and mouth.

9. Place on a lightly greased oven tray and bake in the oven on a moderate setting for 15 minutes.

10. Allow the gingerbread man to cool —

    THEN EAT HIM BEFORE HE RUNS AWAY!

NOTE: You can shape one large gingerbread man, or make a number of smaller gingerbread men, depending on the size of your cutter (for more gingerbread men, you will need more currants and glacé cherries).